14/22

ME and MUHAMMAD ALI

JABARI ASIM *illustrated by* AG FORD

Nancy Paulsen Books

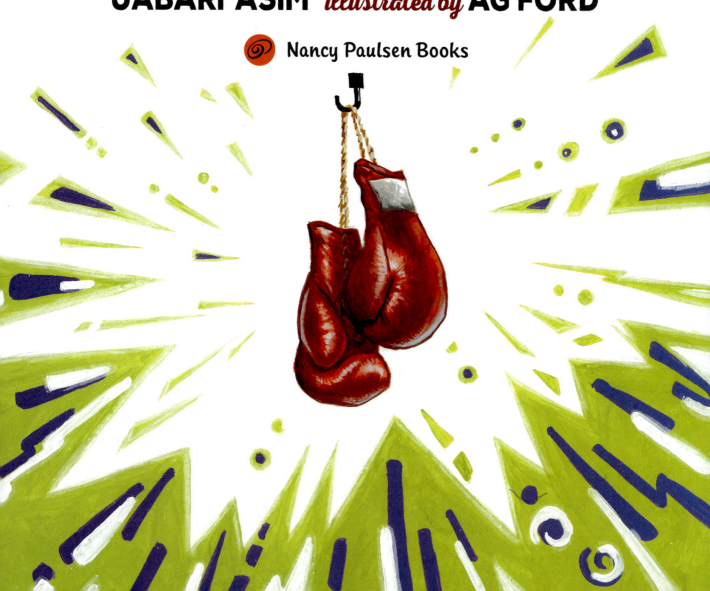

NANCY PAULSEN BOOKS

An imprint of Penguin Random House LLC, New York

First published in the United States of America by Nancy Paulsen Books,
an imprint of Penguin Random House LLC, 2022

Visit us online at penguinrandomhouse.com

Library of Congress Cataloging-in-Publication Data
Names: Asim, Jabari, 1962– author. | Ford, AG, illustrator.
Title: Me and Muhammad Ali / Jabari Asim; [illustrated by AG Ford].
Description: New York: Nancy Paulsen Books, [2022] | Summary: Langston's joyous encounter with
his hero, boxing champion and poet Muhammad Ali, is everything he dreamed it would be and more.
Identifiers: LCCN 2022002118 (print) | LCCN 2022002119 (ebook) | ISBN 9781524739881 (hardcover) |
ISBN 9781524739911 (kindle edition) | ISBN 9781524739898 (epub)
Subjects: CYAC: Ali, Muhammad, 1942–2016—Fiction. | Heroes—Fiction. |
African Americans—Fiction. | LCGFT: Picture books.
Classification: LCC PZ7.A834 Me 2022 (print) | LCC PZ7.A834 (ebook) | DDC [E]—dc23
LC record available at https://lccn.loc.gov/2022002118
LC ebook record available at https://lccn.loc.gov/2022002119

Manufactured in China
ISBN 9781524739881
10 9 8 7 6 5 4 3 2 1
TOPL

Edited by Nancy Paulsen · Art direction by Cecilia Yung · Design by Suki Boynton
Text set in Circe Slab A · The art was done in acrylics and colored pencil on illustration board.

In memory of my mother —JA

To all the leaders in our communities
striving to be role models to our youth —AGF

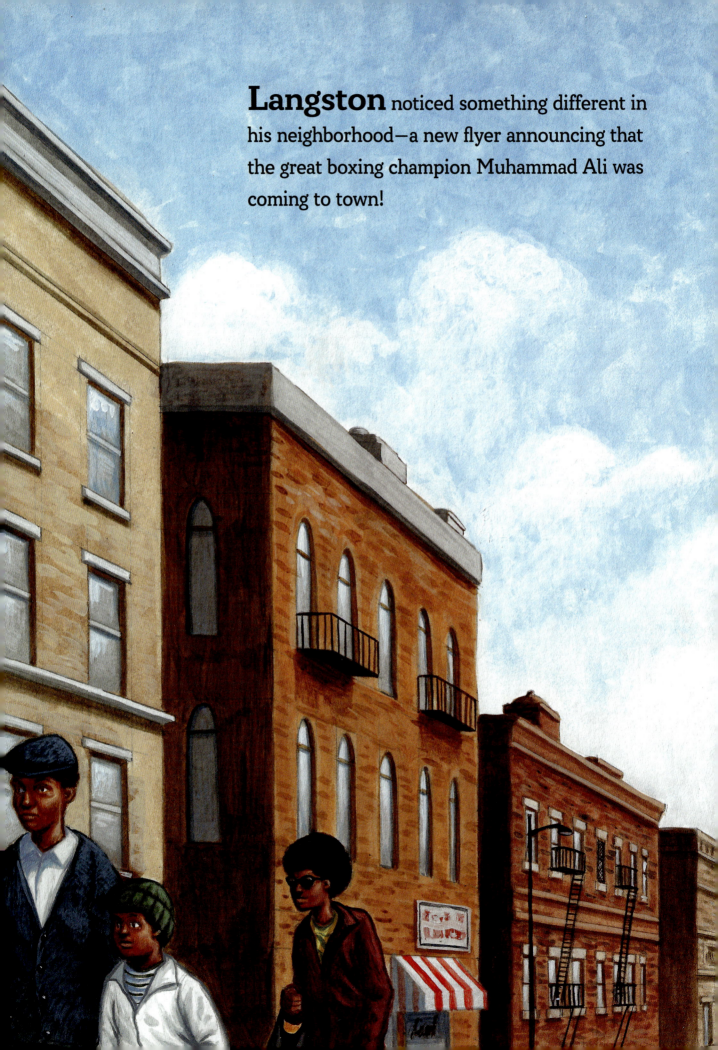

Langston noticed something different in his neighborhood—a new flyer announcing that the great boxing champion Muhammad Ali was coming to town!

The flyer was in front of a large
mural called the Wall of Respect that
Langston's dad had helped paint.

The wall featured the faces of many Black heroes, including Langston's favorite—Muhammad Ali. And now the *real* Muhammad Ali—the champion of the whole world—would actually be here!

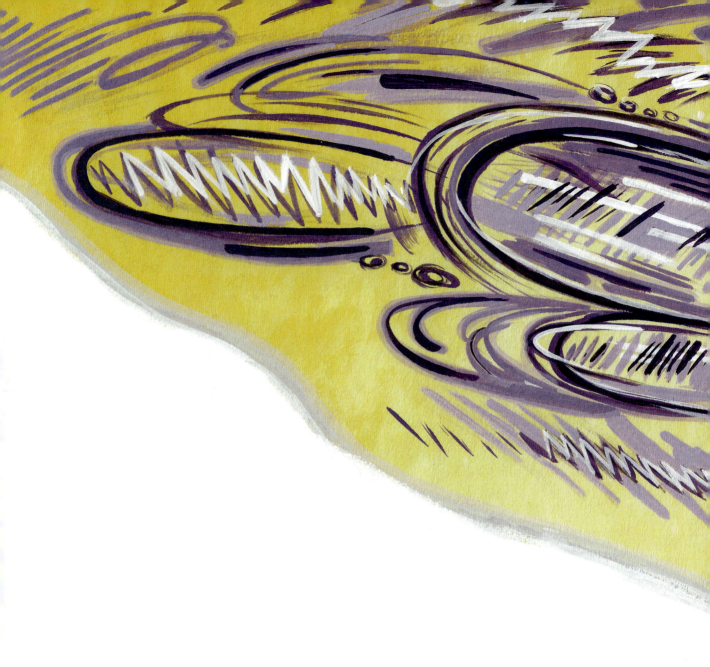

Like most folks, Langston looked up to the champ because of his strength, speed, and confidence. But Langston loved him just as much for his poetry. He was thrilled when Ali promised to float like a butterfly and sting like a bee.

He was delighted
whenever Ali boasted,

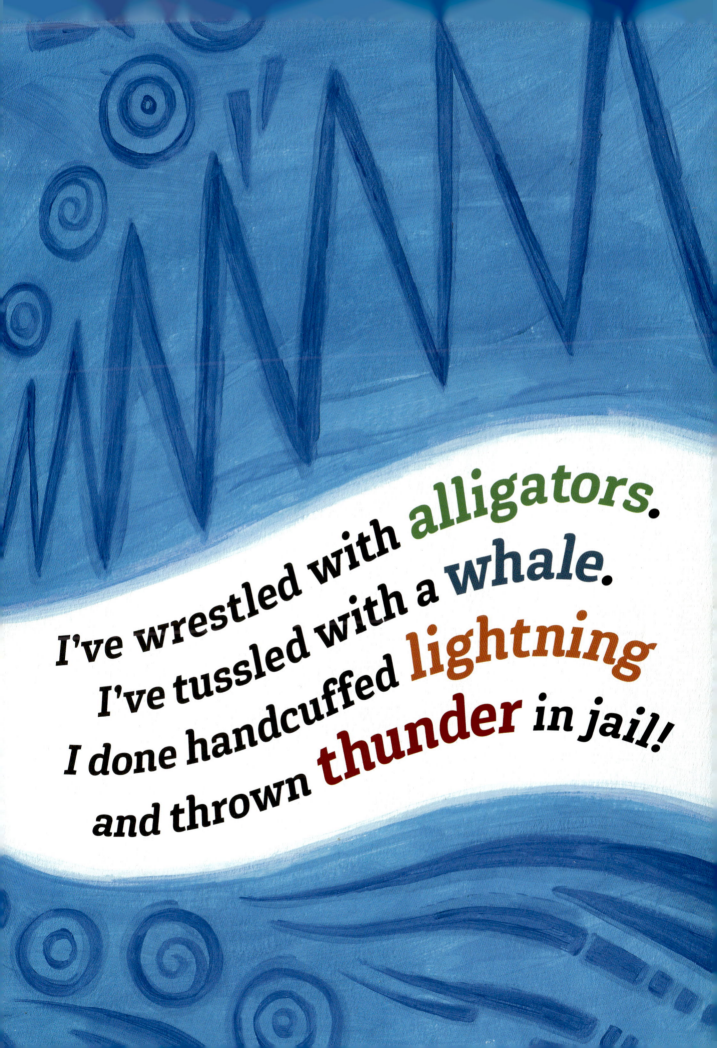

I've wrestled with alligators.
I've tussled with a whale.
I done handcuffed lightning
and thrown thunder in jail!

At recess, the kids were inspired
to make up their own rhymes as they
gathered on the playground. Langston
called up all the confidence he had
and belted out his rhyme:

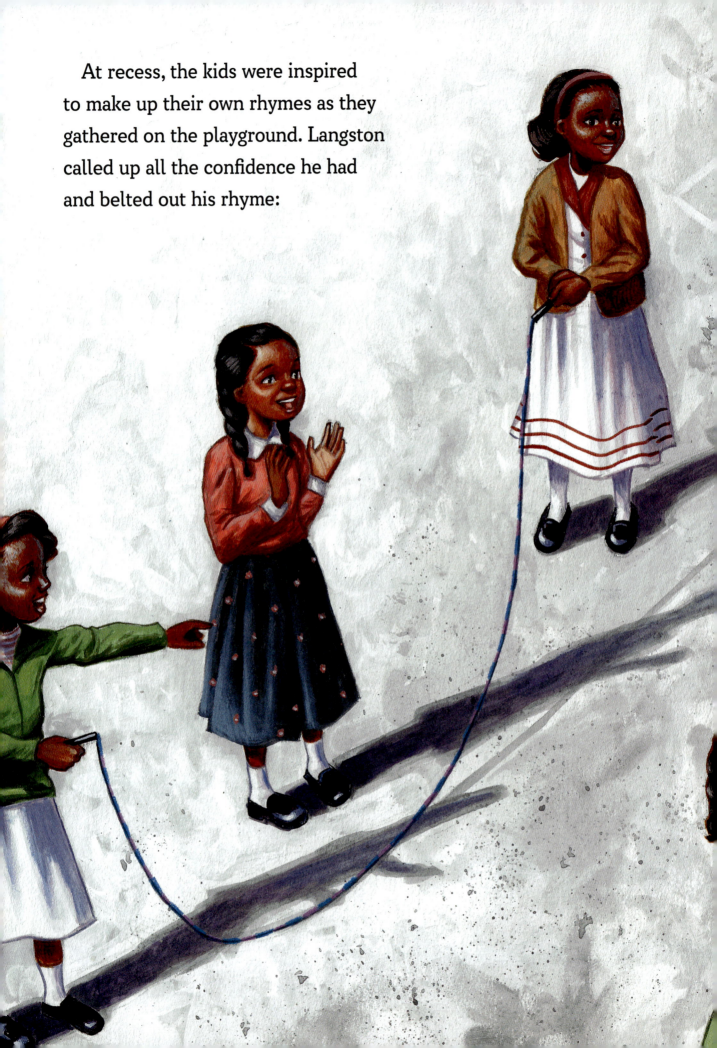

I'm smart as a fox
and fast as a hound.
I can sneak up on you
without making a sound.

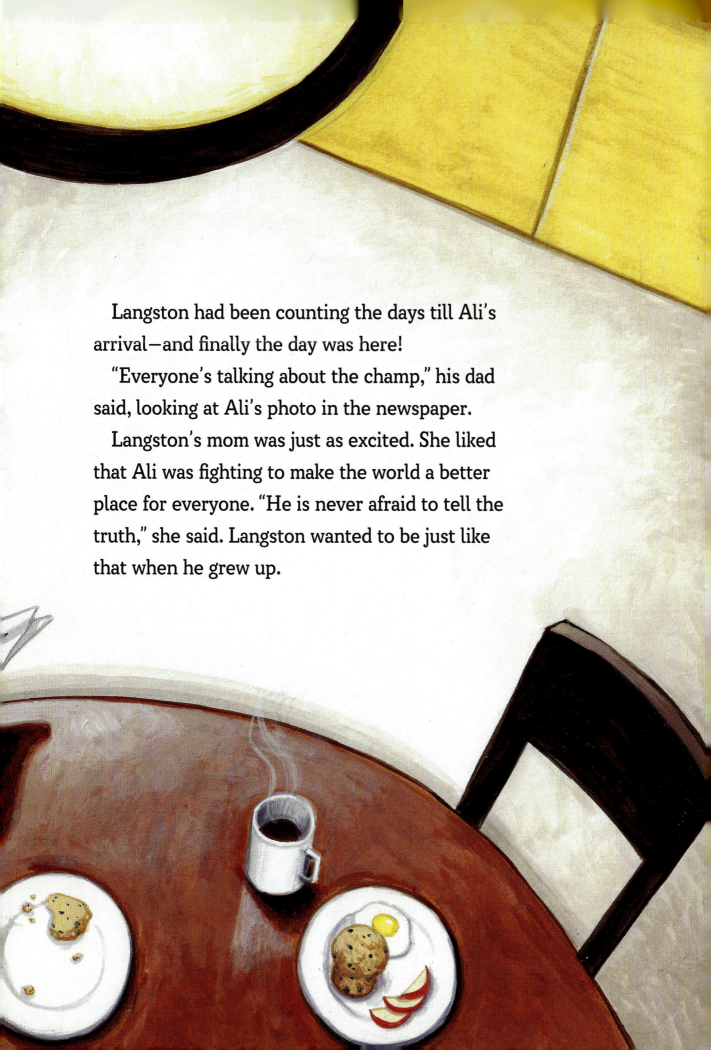

Langston had been counting the days till Ali's arrival—and finally the day was here!

"Everyone's talking about the champ," his dad said, looking at Ali's photo in the newspaper.

Langston's mom was just as excited. She liked that Ali was fighting to make the world a better place for everyone. "He is never afraid to tell the truth," she said. Langston wanted to be just like that when he grew up.

After breakfast, Langston went to the barbershop and got his Afro shaped to look just like the champ's.

He laughed while the old men swapped stories of their younger days. Mr. Sutton, the barber, had even been an athlete himself.

On the wall was a picture of Mr. Sutton receiving a gold medal. He stood on a box with a garland of leaves around his head, near portraits of Jersey Joe Walcott, Henry Armstrong, and other champions Mr. Sutton had known and admired.

"Ali combines the best of all of them," Mr. Sutton told Langston. "I was there when he took the crown from Sonny Liston in '64. Fastest hands I've ever seen." Everyone laughed as Mr. Sutton and Langston pretended to trade punches.

As Langston and his mom left for the high school,
Mr. Sutton yelled out, "Tell the Greatest I said hello."
"I sure will," Langston promised.

Then Langston practically floated like a butterfly
down the street, dreaming of his hero.

At the high school, a guard stopped them. "I'm sorry," he said. "This event is for students only."

"But we're neighbors," Langston's mom said. "We live around the corner. Won't you please let us in?"

"Sorry, ma'am," the guard replied.

"Wait!" Langston said. "You gotta let us in! We've been counting down the days. I even got my Afro trimmed. *Please!*"

The guard just shook his head.

MUHAMMAD ALI
BOXING CHAMPION OF THE WORLD

Then a voice boomed,
"What's the problem here?"
Langston looked up and
could not believe his eyes.

It was **Muhammad Ali**,
the world champion himself.

When the champ heard about their problem, he put his arms around Langston and his mom and told the guard, "Don't worry. They're with me."

Langston could hardly believe their luck!

They all went in together while reporters shouted questions and flashbulbs popped.

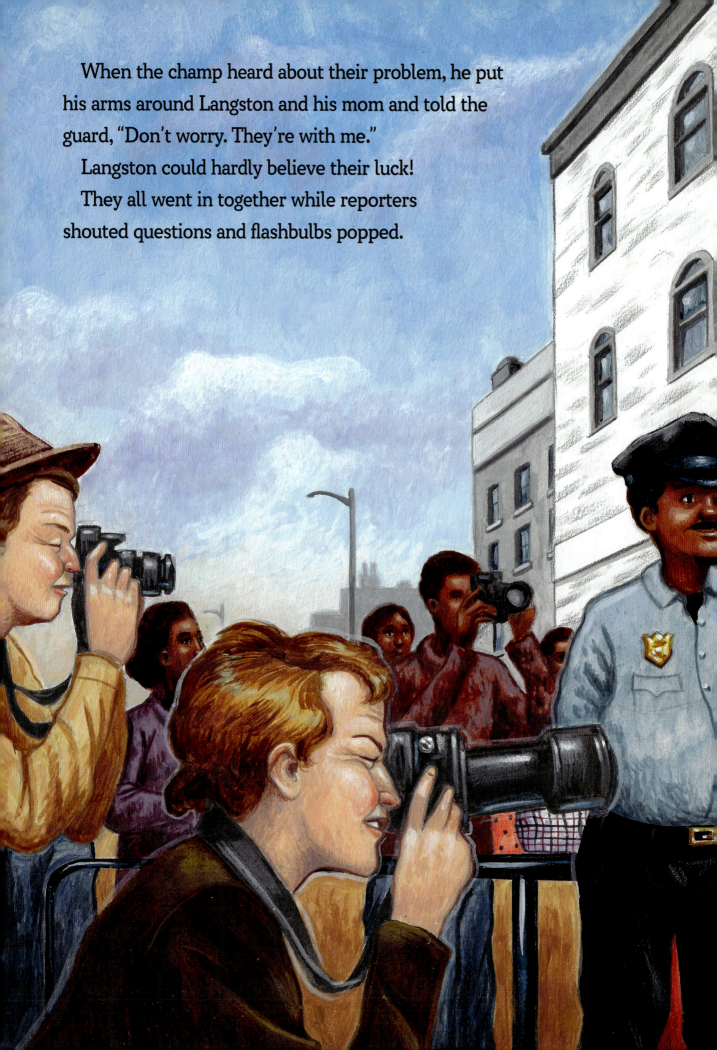

Langston felt joyous and proud,
like Ali strutting in the ring.

The next morning, Langston could still feel
the champ's energy wrapping him in its warm glow.
His hero's face beamed at him as he walked by the
Wall of Respect.

He was already thinking of recess, when he
would tell everyone about meeting the champ.
Then he would chant some rhymes loud enough
for the whole playground to hear.

I'm quick and I'm strong.
I'm Black and I'm free.
I'm brave and I'm bold,
like MUHAMMAD ALI!

AUTHOR'S NOTE

MUHAMMAD ALI was a hero not only to me but also to my entire community. He thrilled us with his athletic grace, his skill in the ring, and his medal-winning excellence. A portrait of him, fists raised high, adorned the Wall of Respect mural in my St. Louis neighborhood.

We also loved him for his fearlessness in challenging racism and opposing the Vietnam War, for his willingness to risk his wealth and fame by speaking truth to power. As unafraid of microphones as he was of his luckless opponents, he could be counted on to deliver an illuminating comment when the times demanded it.

Like many young men of my generation, I followed his career with enthusiasm. I routinely grabbed copies of *Sports Illustrated* in which he appeared, and probably never missed an issue of *Ebony* magazine that featured him and his family.

I also read his memoir, *The Greatest: My Own Story*. It was published in 1975, the same year as the real-life event that inspired this book. When Ali visited a school in my neighborhood, my mom strolled over to get a front-row seat. At the doors, the security personnel told her that the function wasn't open to the public. She was arguing with the guards when Ali himself walked up and asked what was going on. After she explained the situation to him, he took her hand and personally escorted her into the school. For days after, holding hands with Ali was all she could talk about.